Let's Make a Rocket

An Ivy and Mack story

T0337568

Written by Rebecca Colby

Illustrated by Gustavo Mazali

Collins

What's in this story?

Listen and say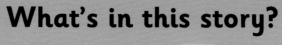

Download the audio at www.collins.co.uk/839778

castle

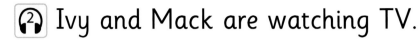 Ivy and Mack are watching TV.

Ivy says, "That's not a box.
It's a castle now!"

6

Mack says, "No! Let's make a rocket."
Ivy says, "Good idea! Let's ask Mum for some old boxes."

Mack is in a box.

Ivy gets some crayons, some glue, some tape and some scissors.

Ivy says, "Mack! Let's start."

Mack says, "How can we make our rocket, Ivy?"

Ivy says, "Here! Take this tape."

Mack asks, "How can we finish our rocket?"

I know.

Ivy says, "Can we have this, Mum?"

Mum says, "Yes, you can. What are you making?"

Mack says, "We're making a rocket."

The children colour the rocket with the crayons. They draw a door and some windows.

Ivy makes some stars for the rocket.

Mack says, "I'm an astronaut.
This is my new rocket."

Mum has an idea. Mum says,
"Find some astronaut clothes."

What are *you* making, Mum?

Mum says, "Here are jetpacks for my two astronauts!"

Dad says, "Look at you! Those old boxes make a good rocket. And those old bottles make great jetpacks!"

Picture dictionary

Listen and repeat

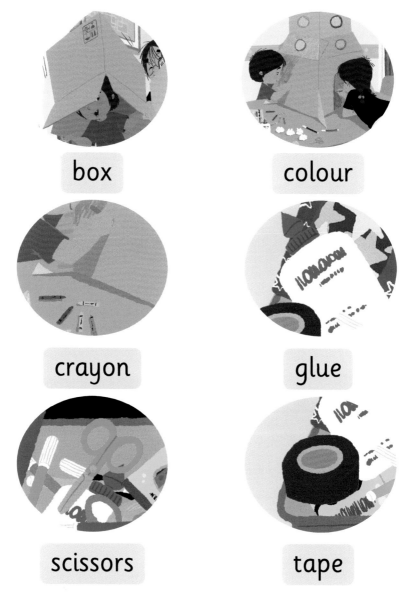

box

colour

crayon

glue

scissors

tape

1 Look and order the story

2 Listen and say

Collins

Published by Collins
An imprint of HarperCollins*Publishers*
Westerhill Road
Bishopbriggs
Glasgow
G64 2QT

HarperCollins*Publishers*
Macken House, 39/40 Mayor Street Upper,
Dublin 1
DO1 C9W8
Ireland

William Collins' dream of knowledge for all began with the publication of his first book in 1819.

A self-educated mill worker, he not only enriched millions of lives, but also founded a flourishing publishing house. Today, staying true to this spirit, Collins books are packed with inspiration, innovation and practical expertise. They place you at the centre of a world of possibility and give you exactly what you need to explore it.

© HarperCollins*Publishers* Limited 2020

10 9 8 7 6 5 4 3

ISBN 978-0-00-839778-4

Collins® and COBUILD® are registered trademarks of HarperCollins*Publishers* Limited

www.collins.co.uk/elt

British Library Cataloguing in Publication Data

A catalogue record for this publication is available from the British Library.

Author: Rebecca Colby
Illustrator: Gustavo Mazali (Beehive)
Series editor: Rebecca Adlard
Publishing manager: Lisa Todd
Product managers: Jennifer Hall and Caroline Green
In-house editor: Alma Puts Keren
Project manager: Emily Hooton
Editor: Deborah Friedland
Proofreaders: Natalie Murray and Michael Lamb
Cover designer: Kevin Robbins
Typesetter: 2Hoots Publishing Services Ltd
Audio produced by id audio, London
Reading guide author: Julie Penn
Production controller: Rachel Weaver
Printed and bound in the UK by Pureprint

MIX
Paper | Supporting responsible forestry
FSC
www.fsc.org
FSC™ C007454

This book contains FSC™ certified paper and other controlled sources to ensure responsible forest management.

For more information visit: www.harpercollins.co.uk/green

Download the audio for this book and a reading guide for parents and teachers at www.collins.co.uk/839778